Ravenscourt
B·O·O·K·S

Monte Cristo's
Prison Years

By
Linda Lott

**Illustrated by
Jeremy Jarvis**

**Based on
The Count of Monte Cristo
by Alexandre Dumas**

Columbus, OH • Chicago, IL • Redmond, WA

The **McGraw·Hill** Companies

SRAonline.com

 SRA

Send all inquiries to:
SRA/McGraw-Hill
8787 Orion Place
Columbus, OH 43240-4027

Printed in the United States of America.

ISBN 0-07-601595-5

4 5 6 7 8 9 MAL 08 07 06 05

Introduction

The Count of Monte Cristo *is the story of Edmond Dantès. This story takes place in France a long time ago. Dantès is a kind, handsome young man. He is about to become the captain of a ship and to be married. He is well liked by most people. However, he has four enemies, including one named Villefort. Some of these men are jealous of Dantès. Some fear that what he knows will ruin them.*

His enemies plot to frame Dantès for treason. An hour before his wedding to Mercédès, Dantès is arrested. At the jail, Dantès is questioned by the prosecutor, Villefort. Villefort decides that Dantès is innocent.

Then Villefort asks to see the letter that caused the problem. Villefort learns that his own father is the traitor. Because he can't let anyone else find out, Villefort burns the letter and promises Dantès that he will be freed.

Of course, this is just a trick to get Dantès out of his office. Villefort is going to send Dantès to prison for the rest of his life. Villefort would be ruined if anyone found out about the letter.

After fourteen years in prison, Dantès will become the Count of Monte Cristo and will get even with his enemies.

This part of the story opens as the guards take Dantès to the prison.

—Chapter 1—

The Prison

In an instant Dantès was placed in a boat between two guards. Soon they were outside the inner harbor.

"Where are you taking me?" Dantès asked.

"We may not tell you."

Strange thoughts passed through his mind. The boat they were in could not make a long trip. There was no ship outside the harbor. Perhaps they were going to leave him on some faraway point. He was not chained. They had not tried to handcuff him. This seemed a good sign. Besides, had not Villefort told him that he had nothing to be afraid of? Had not Dantès seen Villefort burn the fatal letter? It was the only proof against him.

*Dantès turned and saw that they had got out to sea. He turned to the nearest guard. "Comrade," said he, "I beg you to tell me where we are going. I am Captain Dantès, a loyal Frenchman. Tell me where you are taking me. I promise you on my honor I will accept my fate."

Then the guard asked, "You are from Marseilles and a sailor, and yet you do not know where you are going?"

"On my honor, I have no idea."

"Unless you cannot see, or have never been outside the harbor, you must know."

"I do not."

"Look round you." Dantès rose and looked forward. Then he saw the black and frowning rock on which stands the* prison.

"The prison?" cried he. "Why are we going there?"

The guards smiled.

4

"I am not going to be jailed," said Dantès. "I have committed no crime. Am I being taken to the prison to be jailed there?"

"It is likely."

"Without any questioning?"

"You have been questioned."

"And so, in spite of Villefort's promises?"

"I do not know what Villefort promised you," said the guard. "I know we are taking you to the prison. But what are you doing? Help, comrades, help!"

Suddenly Dantès sprang forward to jump into the sea. But four arms grabbed him. He fell back screaming with rage.

"Good!" said the guard, placing his knee on Dantès' chest. "If you move, I will blow your brains out." And he pointed his gun at Dantès' temple.

For a time the idea of struggling crossed Dantès' mind. But he remembered Villefort's promise.

Then the boat got to a landing. His guards forced him to rise. They dragged him toward the steps that led to the gate of the prison.

Dantès was like a man in a dream. He saw soldiers on the wall. He knew that he was going up a flight of steps. He knew that he passed through a door. He knew that the door closed behind him. But it was like looking through a mist.

They stood for nearly ten minutes. They seemed to be waiting for orders. The orders came.

"Where is the prisoner?" asked a voice.

"Here," answered the guards.

"Let him follow me; I will take him to his cell."

"Go!" said the guards, pushing Dantès forward.

The guard led Dantès into a room almost underground. Its bare and stinking walls seemed soaked with tears. A lamp lit the room faintly.

"Here is your room for tonight," said the jailer. "It is late, and the governor is asleep. Tomorrow, perhaps, he might change you. In the meantime there is bread, water, and fresh straw. That is all a prisoner can wish for. Good night." The jailer left with the lamp and closed the door. Dantès was alone in the dark and the cold.

—Chapter 2—

A Worse Place

*In the morning the jailer returned. He had orders to leave Dantès where he was. He found the prisoner in the same place, as if fixed there. Dantès' eyes were swollen with weeping. He had passed the night standing and without sleep.

The jailer touched Dantès on the shoulder.

"Have you not slept?" said the jailer.

"I do not know," answered Dantès. The jailer stared.

"Are you hungry?" continued he.

"I do not know."

"Do you wish for anything?"

"I wish to see the governor."

The jailer shrugged his shoulders. "What you ask is impossible. But if you are very well behaved, you will be allowed to walk about. Someday you will meet the governor, and he might talk to* you."

"But," asked Dantès, "how long shall I have to wait?"

"Ah, a month—six months—a year."

"It is too long a time. I wish to see him at once."

"Ah," said the jailer, "do not always think about the impossible, or you will be mad in two weeks."

"You think so?"

"Yes. The abbot who was in this cell before you went mad. He offered the government a million francs for his freedom."

"How long since he left it?"

"Two years."

"Was he set free, then?"

"No. He was put in a dungeon."

"Listen!" said Dantès. "I am not an abbot. I am not mad. Perhaps I shall be, but for now, I am not. I will make you another offer."

"What is that?"

"I do not offer you a million francs because I have it not. I will give you a hundred francs. The first time you go to Marseilles, you must find a young girl named Mercédès and give her a note from me."

"If I took the francs and were discovered, I would lose my job. It is worth two thousand francs a year. I would be a great fool to run such a risk for a hundred."

"Well," said Dantès, "remember this. I will someday hide myself behind the door, and when you enter I will dash out your brains with this stool."

"Threats!" cried the jailer. "You are going mad. The abbot began like you. In three days you will be mad like him. Luckily, there are dungeons here." Dantès whirled the stool round his head.

"All right, all right," said the jailer. " I will send word to the governor."

"Very well," said Dantès, dropping the stool.

The jailer went out and returned with five soldiers.

"By the governor's orders," said he, "take the prisoner to the floor below."

"To the dungeon, then," said a soldier.

"Yes. We must put the madman with the madmen." The soldiers grabbed Dantès, who followed quietly.

He went down fifteen steps. The door of a dungeon was opened, and he was pushed in. The door closed. Dantès moved forward until he touched the wall. He then sat down in the corner until his eyes became used to the darkness. The jailer was right. Dantès was very nearly mad.

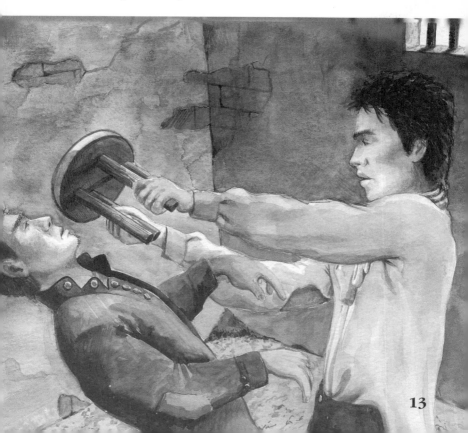

—Chapter 3—

The Two Prisoners

A year later, the inspector of prisons made a visit to the prison. He visited the cells and dungeons of many of the prisoners. He asked how they were fed and whether they had any needs. They all answered that the food was terrible and that they wanted to be set free.

"I do not know why I have to make these useless visits. When you see one prisoner, you see all. Always the same thing, ill-fed and innocent. Are there any others?"

"Yes. The mad prisoners are in the dungeons."

"Let us visit them," said the inspector. "We must play this joke to the end. Let us see the dungeons."

*"Let us first send for two soldiers," said the governor. "The prisoners are sometimes violent."

Two soldiers were sent for. The inspector moved down a stinking, damp, dark stairway.

"Oh," cried the inspector, "who can live here?"

"A most dangerous traitor. We are ordered to keep a strict watch over him. He is daring and stubborn."

"He is alone?"

"Yes."

"How long has he been there?"

"Nearly a year. Now we have an abbot in another dungeon. He has been here since 1811, and in 1813 he went mad. You had better see him."

"I will see them both," answered the inspector.

"Let us visit this one first," added he.

"By all means," answered the governor. He signed to the* turnkey to open the door.

Dantès sat in a corner of the dungeon. He raised his head. He sprang forward with clasped hands.

"I want to know what crime I have committed. I want to be tried. If I am guilty, I want to be shot. If I'm innocent, I want to be set free."

"Are you well fed?" said the inspector.

"I believe so. I do not know. It does not matter. What matters is that an innocent man has to die in prison."

"You are very mild today," said the governor.

"Being in prison has quieted me. I have been here so long."

"So long? When were you arrested, then?" asked the inspector.

"The 28th of February, 1815, at half past two in the afternoon."

"Today is the 30th of July, 1816. Why, it is but seventeen months."

"Only seventeen months," answered Dantès. "Oh, you do not know what is seventeen months in prison! I ask only for a trial. Surely you must do that!"

"We shall see," said the inspector.

"Oh, I am free. Then I am saved!"

"Who arrested you?"

"Villefort. See him, and hear what he says."

"Villefort is no longer at Marseilles. He is now at Toulouse."

"Then I am no longer surprised," whispered Dantès. "My only help is gone."

"Did Villefort hate you?"

"Oh, no. He was very kind to me."

"I can, then, count on the notes he has left about you?"

"Yes."

"That is well." The door closed.

"Will you see the records," asked the governor, "or go to the other cells?"

"Let us visit them all now," said the inspector. "Once I go up those stairs, I will not have the courage to come down again."

"This next prisoner has the madness. He thinks he has a huge treasure. The first year he offered the government a million francs to be set free. The second, two; the third, three; and so on. He is now in his fifth year in prison. He will ask to speak to you and offer you five million."

"How strange! What is his name?"

"The Abbot Faria. Here he is. Number 27," said the governor.

In the center of the cell sat a man whose tattered clothes barely covered him.

"What is it you want?" said the inspector.

"I, sir," answered Faria, "I want nothing."

"You do not understand," continued the inspector. "I am sent here by government to visit the prisoners and hear what they need."

"Oh, that is different," cried Faria. "And we shall understand each other, I hope. I wish to tell you about an important treasure. The government may have it all."

"My dear sir, the government is rich and does not want your treasures," answered the inspector. "Keep them until you are freed."

Faria's eyes flashed. He grabbed the inspector's hand. "But what if I am not freed?" cried he. "This treasure will be lost. I will offer six million. Just give me my freedom."

"On my word," said the inspector in a low tone, "had I not been told that this man was mad, I would believe what he says."

"I am not mad," answered Faria. "There is a treasure. I offer to sign an agreement with you. I promise to lead you to the spot where you shall dig. If I am not telling the truth, return me to prison."

"I asked whether you are well fed," said the inspector.

"Promise me," answered Faria. "Free me if what I tell you is true."

"Are you well fed?" asked the inspector again.

"Sir, you run no risk. I will stay here. There is no chance of my escaping."

"You do not answer my question," said the inspector.

"Nor you mine," cried Faria. "You will not accept my gold. I will keep it for myself. You refuse me my freedom. God will give it me."

The inspector kept his word with Dantès. Later he examined the records and found the following note:

Edmond Dantès:
Violent traitor.
Use the greatest care.

There was nothing the inspector could do. He wrote, "Nothing to be done."

At the end of a year the governor was moved. A new governor arrived. It would have been hard for him to learn the names of the prisoners. He learned their numbers instead. The unhappy young man was no longer Edmond Dantès. He was now number 34.

—Chapter 4—

Number 34 and Number 27

Nearly four years passed away. At the end of the second, Dantès had stopped marking time.

Dantès said, "I wish to die." He decided to starve himself. "When my morning and evening meals are brought," thought he, "I will cast them out the window. They will think that I have eaten them."

He kept his word. Twice a day he threw out his food. He did this until he did not have enough strength to rise. The next morning he could not see or hear. The jailer feared he was ill. Dantès hoped he was dying.

About nine o'clock in the evening, Dantès heard a sound in the wall against which he was lying.

*Dantès raised his head and listened. It was a continual scratching. The sound lasted nearly three hours. Then Dantès heard the noise of something falling. At last, all was silent.

Some hours later it began again. Suddenly the jailer entered.

The jailer brought him his breakfast. Dantès began to talk about everything. He had to keep the jailer from hearing the scratching.

The jailer placed the food on the table and left. Dantès listened. The sound became clearer.

"There can be no doubt about it," thought he. "It is some prisoner trying to dig out. Oh, if I were only there to help him!"

Then he said to himself, "If it is a prisoner, the noise I make will alarm* him. He will stop and not begin again until he thinks everyone is asleep."

Dantès went to a corner of his dungeon. He removed a stone and with it knocked against the wall where the sound came. He struck three times. At the first blow the sound stopped.

Dantès listened. An hour passed. Two hours passed. No sound was heard from the wall.

The day passed away in silence. The night passed in perfect silence. Dantès did not close his eyes.

Three days passed. One evening Dantès heard a faint movement. Something was at work on the other side of the wall.

Dantès decided that he had to help the other prisoner. He began by moving his bed. He tried to find something to use to remove a stone. He saw nothing. There was only one thing Dantès could do. He dropped a jug, and it broke into pieces.

Dantès hid the sharpest pieces in his bed. He could not do much in the night because of the darkness. He pushed back his bed and waited for day.

All night he heard the workman. After the jailer brought his food in the morning, Dantès moved his bed. He saw that his work had been useless. He had been attacking the stone instead of the plaster around it.

Dantès began to work. Because the plaster was damp, Dantès could break it off in small pieces. At this rate, it would take him two years to dig a passage.

Then Dantès had an idea. The jailer always brought Dantès' soup in an iron pan. The handle of this pan was iron. Dantès would have given ten years of his life for it.

That evening Dantès tricked the jailer into leaving the pan. Dantès quickly ate his food. He moved his bed. Then he put the handle of the pan between two stones of the wall and used it as a lever. At the end of an hour, a stone was out of the wall. It left a hole a foot and a half across.

Dantès collected the plaster. He carried it into the corner of his cell and covered it with earth. Then he continued to work. In the morning he put the stone back. He pushed his bed against the wall and lay down.

After Dantès had been working for several nights, he hit something. Dantès touched it. He found that it was a beam. This beam crossed the hole Dantès had made. He had to dig above or under it.

"O my God, my God!" whispered he. "Is there no hope? Do not let this be!"

"Who talks of God and lost hope at the same time?" said a voice that seemed to come from the earth. Dantès' hair stood on end. He rose to his knees.

"In the name of heaven," cried Dantès, "speak again. Who are you?"

"Who are you?" said the voice.

"An unhappy prisoner," answered Dantès.

"Of what country?"

"A Frenchman."

"Your name?"

"Edmond Dantès."

"Your job?"

"A sailor."

"How long have you been here?"

"Since the 28th of February, 1815."

"Your crime?"

"I am innocent."

"But with what were you charged?"

"Of having plotted to help Napoleon return. How long have you been here?" asked Dantès.

"Since 1811. Do not dig anymore," said the voice, "only tell me how high up is the hole?"

"On a level with the floor."

"How is it hidden?"

"Behind my bed."

"Has your bed been moved since you have been a prisoner?"

"No."

"What does your cell open on?"

"A hallway."

"And the hallway?"

"On a court."

"I have made a mistake," said the voice. "I took a wrong turn. I thought the wall you are mining was the outer wall of the prison."

"But then you would be close to the sea?"

"That is what I hoped. I would have thrown myself into the sea. I would have swum to one of the islands near here. Then I would have been safe."

"Could you have swum so far?"

"Yes. Stop up the hole carefully. Do not work anymore until you hear from me."

"Tell me, at least, who you are?"

"I am—I am number 27."

"You do not trust me, then," said Dantès.

"How old are you? Your voice is that of a young man."

"I do not know my age. I have not counted the years I have been here. All I do know is that I was just nineteen when I was arrested, the 28th of February, 1815."

"Not quite twenty-six!" whispered the voice. "At that age you cannot be a traitor."

"Oh, no, no," cried Dantès. "Rather than betray you, I would allow myself to be hacked in pieces!"

"You have done well to speak to me. I was about to form another plan. I will not forget you. Wait."

"How long?"

"I must figure out our chances. I will give you the signal."

"But you will not leave me. You will come to me, or you will let me come to you. We will escape. If we cannot escape, we will talk," Dantès said.

"It is well," returned the voice. "Tomorrow."

The next morning, as Dantès removed his bed from the wall, he heard three knocks.

"Is it you?" said he. "I am here."

"Is your jailer gone?"

"Yes," said Dantès. "He will not return until the evening. We have twelve hours before us."

"I can work, then?" said the voice.

"Oh, yes, yes. This instant, I beg you."

In time, part of the floor gave way. From the bottom of the hole, Dantès saw first the head, then the shoulders, and lastly the body of a man, who sprang lightly into his cell.

Chapter 5

The Treasure

For eight years Dantès and the other prisoner, Abbot Faria, meet in secret. During this time they plan their escape. Faria also uses this time to teach Dantès history, science, psychology, and several languages.

During their talks, Faria helps Dantès figure out why he is in prison and who is to blame. After Faria becomes ill, he cannot carry out the escape. He tells Dantès that he must go on without him. Dantès refuses to leave his friend. Because Dantès has been a true and loyal friend, Faria decides to tell him about the treasure hidden on the Island of Monte Cristo and how to find it. The treasure had belonged to the Spada family.

*"But," asked Dantès, "has this treasure no owner in the world?"

"No, no, be easy on that score. The family is dead. The last Count of Spada made me his heir. If we lay hands on this treasure, we may enjoy it without guilt."

"And you say this treasure is worth . . ."

"Two million Roman crowns, nearly thirteen million of our money."

"Impossible!" said Dantès.

"Impossible? And why?" asked the old man. "The Spada family was one of the oldest and most powerful families."

Dantès thought he was in a dream.

"I have only kept this secret so long from you," continued Faria, "that I might test you and then surprise you. Had we escaped before my illness, I would have* taken you to Monte Cristo. Now it is you who will take me there. Well, Dantès, you do not thank me?"

"This treasure belongs to you, my dear friend, and to you only. I have no right to it. I am not your son."

"You are my son, Dantès," said the old man. "You are the child of my prison years. God has sent you to me."

—Chapter 6—

Escape

One night Dantès woke up suddenly. He thought someone was calling him. He opened his eyes upon utter darkness. The call came from Faria's dungeon. "Can it be?" whispered Dantès.

He moved his bed. Then he drew up the stone and rushed into the passage. When he reached the other end, the secret entrance was open. Dantès saw the old man, clinging to the bed.

"My dear friend," said Faria, "you understand. I need not tell you?"

Dantès uttered a cry. He rushed toward the door, yelling, "Help, help!" Faria had just enough strength to stop him.

"Silence," he said, "or you are lost. We must now think only of you, my dear friend."

*Dantès could only clasp his hands and cry, "Oh, my friend, my friend, do not speak this way!"

"There is no hope," answered Faria, shaking his head. "Now lift me on my bed, for I can no longer support myself."

Dantès took the old man in his arms and placed him on the bed.

"And now, my dear friend," said Faria, "I wish you happiness and riches. My son, I bless you!" The young man fell on his knees, leaning his head against the old man's bed.

"Listen, now, to what I say. There really is a treasure. If you do escape, remember that the poor abbot, whom all the world called mad, was not so. Hurry to Monte Cristo.* Find the treasure, for you have suffered long enough." A violent fit attacked the old man.

"Good-bye," whispered the old man, clasping Dantès' hand. "Good-bye!"

"Oh, no, no, not yet," Dantès cried. "Do not leave me! Help! Help! Help!"

"Hush, hush!" whispered the dying man. And raising himself, he said, "Monte Cristo, forget not Monte Cristo!" And he fell back.

Half an hour, an hour, an hour and a half went by. Dantès leaned over his friend. He felt the body grow cold. The heart's beat became deeper and dull, until it stopped. It was six o'clock in the morning.

Dantès put out the lamp and hid it. Then he went away, closing as well as he could the entrance to the secret passage.

It was time; the jailer was coming. He began his rounds at Dantès' cell, and then he went on to Faria's dungeon.

Dantès wanted to know what was going on in the dungeon of his friend. He sneaked through the passage. He arrived in time to hear the turnkey call out for help. Other turnkeys came. Last of all came the governor.

Dantès heard the creaking of the bed as they moved the body. He heard them send for the doctor. It seemed to him as if everyone had left the cell. Still he did not dare to enter, as they might have left some turnkey to watch the dead. He remained in the tunnel, hardly breathing.

At the end of an hour, he heard a faint noise, which grew louder. It was the governor who returned, followed by the doctor and others. There was silence. The doctor was examining the dead body.

"You may make your mind easy," said the doctor. "He is dead. I will answer for that. I hope that you will treat him properly."

"Yes, yes. He shall be buried in the newest sack we can find. Will that do?"

Other footsteps, going and coming, were heard. Then the noise of rustling canvas reached Dantès' ears. The bed creaked. The heavy footfall of a man who lifts a weight sounded on the floor. Then the bed again creaked under the weight dropped on it.

"This evening," said the governor.

"Will there be any mass?"

"No," answered the governor.

Meanwhile the men were putting the body in the sack.

"This evening," said the governor, when the task was ended.

"At what hour?" asked a turnkey.

"Why, about ten or eleven o'clock."

"Shall we watch the body?"

"Of what use would it be? Shut the dungeon as if he were alive." Then the voices died away. Dantès raised the stone and looked carefully around the cell. It was empty, and Dantès came out of the tunnel.

He lifted his hand to his head as if his brain were mad.

"Just God," he whispered, "where does this thought come from? Is it from you? None but the dead pass from this dungeon. Let me take the place of the dead!"

Without giving himself time to think, he bent over the sack. He opened it with the knife that Faria had made. He took the body from the sack and carried it along the tunnel to his own cell. He laid it on his bed and covered it with his blanket. He kissed the old man. Then he turned Faria's head toward the wall so that the jailer might believe that he was asleep.

Then Dantès entered the tunnel again. He pulled the bed against the wall. He returned to the other cell and took from the hiding place the needle and thread. He got inside the sack. Then he sewed up the mouth of the sack from the inside.

If the grave diggers took him to the grave, he would allow himself to be covered with earth. Then he would work his way through the earth and escape.

Footsteps were heard on the stairs. Dantès felt that the time had arrived. He held his breath. The footsteps stopped at the door. The door opened. A dim light reached Dantès' eyes through the rough sack that covered him. He saw two shadows come to his bed. A third remained at the door. The two men lifted the sack.

"He's heavy for an old and thin man," said one, as he raised the head.

"They say every year adds half a pound to the weight of the bones," said another.

"Have you tied the knot?" asked the first speaker.

"What would be the use of carrying so much more weight?" was the answer. "I can do that when we get there."

"What's the knot for?" thought Dantès.

They placed Dantès' body on the bier. Dantès stiffened himself to play a dead man.

Suddenly he felt the fresh and sharp night air. The bearers went on for twenty paces and then stopped. One of them went away.

"Give us a light," said one bearer. "I shall never find what I am looking for."

"What can he be looking for?" thought Dantès. "The spade, perhaps."

"Here it is at last," the bearer said, "not without some trouble though."

"Yes," was the answer, "but it has lost nothing by waiting."

As he said this, the man came toward Dantès, who heard something metal laid down beside him, and at the same time a cord was fastened round his feet with a sudden and painful jerk.

"Well, have you tied the knot?" asked the other bearer, who was looking on.

"Yes, and pretty tight too, I can tell you," was the answer.

"Move on, then." The body was lifted from the bier once more, and they went on.

They went fifty paces farther, and then stopped to open a door. They went forward again. The noise of the waves dashing against the rocks reached Dantès' ears.

"Bad weather!" said one of the bearers. "Not a good night for a dip in the sea."

"Well, here we are at last," said one of them.

"A little farther," said the other. "You know the last was stopped on his way, dashed on the rocks."

They went down five or six more steps. Then Dantès felt that they took him, one by the head and the other by the heels, and swung him to and fro. "One!" said the "grave diggers." "Two! Three!" And at the same instant Dantès felt himself flung into the air.

Dantès had been flung into the sea and was dragged into the deep by a thirty-six pound weight tied to his feet. The sea is the graveyard of the prison.